PUFFIN BOOKS

Ricky, Zedex and the Spooks

Frank Rodgers was formerly an art teacher but is now a full-time illustrator and author. He is married with two children and lives in Glasgow.

D1101102

Other books by Frank Rodgers

THE INTERGALACTIC KITCHEN
THE INTERGALACTIC KITCHEN GOES PREHISTORIC
RICKY'S SUMMERTIME CHRISTMAS PRESENT
TEACHERS . . . OR CREATURES?

Ricky, Zedex and the Spooks

Frank Rodgers

PUFFIN BOOKS

PUFFIN BOOKS

Published by the Penguin Group
Penguin Books Ltd, 27 Wrights Lane, London W8 5TZ, England
Penguin Books USA Inc., 375 Hudson Street, New York, New York 10014, USA
Penguin Books Australia Ltd, Ringwood, Victoria, Australia
Penguin Books Canada Ltd, 10 Alcorn Avenue, Toronto, Ontario, Canada M4V 3B2
Penguin Books (NZ) Ltd, 182–190 Wairau Road, Auckland 10, New Zealand

Penguin Books Ltd, Registered Offices: Harmondsworth, Middlesex, England

First published by Viking 1992
Published in Puffin Books 1994
3 5 7 9 10 8 6 4 2

Copyright © Frank Rodgers, 1992
All rights reserved

The moral right of the author/illustrator has been asserted

Filmset in Times (Linotron 202)
Printed in England by Clays Ltd, St Ives plc

Except in the United States of America, this book is sold subject to the condition that it shall not, by way of trade or otherwise, be lent, re-sold, hired out, or otherwise circulated without the publisher's prior consent in any form of binding or cover other than that in which it is published and without a similar condition including this condition being imposed on the subsequent purchaser

Chapter One

It was dark, and Ricky Brown was crawling round his Uncle Jack's garden in the country. Beside him was his friend Zedex, the robot that he had built with his uncle. He and Zedex were helping Uncle Jack gather information about the habits of nocturnal creatures and were on the track of a badger.

"Look!" whispered Ricky, pointing to a shape moving beneath the shrubbery. "There it is!"

Zedex turned towards the small animal and pressed a few buttons on his chest-mounted computer-console.

Ricky heard a quiet hum as Zedex's built-in, infra-red camera started to take video pictures of the badger as it snuffled around, looking for insects.

Ricky could just make out the badger's black and white markings in the gloom, but he knew that Zedex's infra-red camera would take clear pictures.

Suddenly something disturbed the badger. It stopped rooting around and sat upright, its nose twitching. Then, quick as a flash, it disappeared into the bushes.

Ricky groaned. "What a shame," he said. "Just as you were getting some good pictures, Zedex. I wonder what disturbed it?"

Just at that moment, a fluttering white shape caught his eye. It was on the bush which the badger had been under and looked like a torn piece of paper caught in a breeze.

Zedex had seen it too and looked up.

"Shall I film it, Ricky?" he asked in his funny, electronic voice.

"Yes, Zedex," said Ricky, "it could be interesting."

As Ricky said that, however, the white shape left the bush, fluttered into the dark sky and disappeared.

"Did you manage to get it, Zedex?" Ricky asked anxiously.

"Yes, Ricky, but only for a few seconds," said Zedex.

They stood up.

"I wonder what on earth it was," Ricky frowned.

"Perhaps we'll find out when I check the videotape," said Zedex.

Uncle Jack was excited by the news.

"This sounds fascinating," he said. "You did well, both of you. But . . ." he stifled a yawn, ". . . it is getting late, so I think we'll leave it until the morning." He yawned again. "Goodnight, you two."

Zedex settled himself in a corner of Ricky's bedroom as Ricky got into bed.

"Ready to switch off now?" asked Zedex.

Ricky laughed. "If you mean am I ready to go to sleep, then yes, I am," he said.

Zedex's face-screen glowed slightly pink with embarrassment. "Sorry," he apologized with a smile. "I keep forgetting that you are not a robot like me."

"And sometimes I forget that you are not human, like me," said Ricky.

Zedex smiled with pleasure.

"Thank you," he said. "Good switch-off . . . oops, I mean goodnight."

"Goodnight," said Ricky, watching Zedex's face-screen go dark as the robot switched off his sensors for the night.

Ricky snuggled down and thought how lucky he was to have an uncle who could invent someone as marvellous as Zedex. He smiled to himself. Uncle Jack was lucky too! After all, Ricky was the one who had put Zedex together. Then he and the clever robot had rescued Uncle Jack when the inventor had been kidnapped. He smiled again as he drifted off into sleep. Perhaps he and Zedex would have another adventure soon?

Next morning, Ricky was wakened by a strange noise.

He blinked, rubbed his eyes and saw that the noise was coming from Zedex.

The robot was still standing in his corner, but across his

face-screen flashed lines and squiggles. A high-pitched, electronic buzzing sound was coming from Zedex's computer-console.

Ricky sat up in bed. "Are you all right, Zedex?" he asked anxiously.

Zedex's face-screen cleared and on it appeared the robot's friendly expression. He smiled.

"I am sorry if I caused you to switch on . . . er . . . I mean wake up, Ricky," he said. "But I've been studying the videotape from last night. I think I may have some interesting news for you and Professor Brown!"

Ricky quickly got dressed and followed Zedex into his uncle's work-room.

Uncle Jack was already there, so he and Ricky waited eagerly as Zedex finished his checking procedure.

"The first thing I have to tell you," said Zedex, "is that the white object we saw last night was a bat."

Uncle Jack's eyebrows shot up.

"A bat? A white bat? Are you sure, Zedex?" he exclaimed.

"Yes," said Zedex, and he showed them a picture of it on his face-screen.

Uncle Jack shook his head in amazement.

"Well I never," he muttered.

"That is not all," said Zedex smugly. "I have saved the most interesting information till last."

"Oh?" said Ricky and Uncle Jack together, and when Zedex didn't continue, they said impatiently, "Well?"

Zedex spoke slowly, an excited look on his face-screen. "Not only is it a white bat," he said, "but it is also a robot!"

Chapter Two

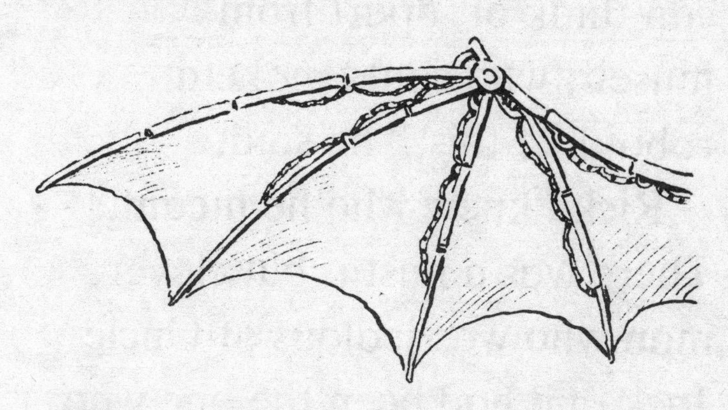

Ricky and Uncle Jack gasped.

"A robot!" they chorused.

Zedex nodded, and on his face-screen there appeared a close-up of the bat's wings. They saw that they were made of thin metal rods, wires and fine plastic.

Uncle Jack frowned.

"There is only one person I can think of, apart from myself, who could make a robot like this," he said.

Ricky knew who he meant. There was a nasty, but clever, man who was jealous of Uncle Jack and had been the one who had kidnapped him.

"Professor Felonius!" he breathed.

His uncle nodded.

"It must be him," he said grimly. "I wonder what he's up to?"

"Perhaps if we wait in the garden tonight, we'll see the

bat again and be able to find out more," Ricky suggested.

"Good idea," said Uncle Jack. "We could follow it to see where it goes."

Ricky and Zedex were the first to go into the garden that evening as darkness fell.

"I'll join you in a few minutes," called Uncle Jack. "I just have to complete a little experiment."

Zedex scanned the night sky with his infra-red vision, but there was no sign of the bat.

Then suddenly they saw it.

It flitted across the end of the garden, but before Zedex could begin filming, it flew off into the countryside.

Ricky looked round quickly, but Uncle Jack was nowhere to be seen.

"Quick, Zedex," he said urgently. "Let's follow it!"

"Good idea, Ricky," said Zedex, who loved the idea of adventure. He quickly flipped down the little seat in his back and Ricky clambered aboard.

Swiftly Zedex adjusted the flight-control on his computer-console.

"All set?" he asked.

"All set!" said Ricky.

"Then off we go," said Zedex, and they soared up into the night sky.

Ricky had flown with Zedex before, but each time was as exciting as the first. He clung on to the robot's shoulders and looked ahead, peering into the dark.

Just then, the moon came out from behind a cloud and bathed the whole countryside in a silvery glow.

Ricky pointed. "There!" he cried.

Not far off, they saw the flickering white shape of the bat as it darted along just above the tree-tops.

Zedex swooped down until he too was flying at the same level.

"Careful," warned Ricky, as

some of the topmost leaves brushed the robot's feet.

Zedex laughed. "It tickles," he said. "My sensors like it."

The bat flew across the open countryside until it came to a main road. There it turned and followed the road, flying low now, just above the hedgerows.

Zedex kept a short distance behind it. Then he and Ricky saw the bat suddenly veer across the road and head for a field, where a number of large trucks were parked.

The back doors of one were slightly open and the bat disappeared inside.

Zedex landed gently beside the trucks and Ricky dismounted.

Quietly they crept up to the truck into which the bat had disappeared. Ricky looked up at its towering bulk. Along its side, in huge white lettering that glowed silver in the moonlight, were the words THE HAUNTED HOUSE.

Ricky gulped and looked around nervously at the dark, looming shapes of the other trucks. Perhaps they were haunted too!

Trying to feel brave, he and Zedex stealthily crept to the back of the truck.

"Shall we look inside?" hissed Zedex, pointing to the slightly open door.

Ricky gulped again and nodded.

Slowly, very slowly, Zedex reached up and eased the door open a bit more.

Suddenly a large, eerie shape rose up from the inside of the truck and hovered above their heads.

Startled, Ricky and Zedex

stumbled backwards and sat down with a bump on the grass.

The white shape still hovered above them, glowing strangely in the dark.

"It . . . it's a ghost!" cried Ricky.

Chapter Three

"What's going on out there?" a deep voice rumbled from the inside of the truck.

A large, jovial man's face appeared round the door and looked in amazement at the two figures sitting on the grass.

"What on earth. . . ?" he began, then burst out laughing.

He climbed out of the truck and Ricky saw that he had a remote-control device in his hand. The man touched a button on it and the "ghost" turned around and flew back into the truck.

Ricky understood.

"It's another robot!" he gasped.

The man laughed again.

"Correct," he said, and winked at Zedex. "Just like your friend here."

Zedex got to his feet and bowed politely.

"Pleased to meet you," he said. "I am ZX 642436/7. Invented by Professor Brown."

"That's my dad's brother, Uncle Jack," Ricky explained. "My name is Ricky and you can call my friend Zedex."

The man shook his hand and bowed to Zedex.

"Delighted," he said. "I'm Stan Bellamy. They call me Stan the Spooksman. I'm part of this funfair, you see," he said and pointed to the other trucks. "I run THE HAUNTED HOUSE and my ambition is to have the most realistic spooks in the world!"

"Your ghost certainly scared me!" Ricky said with a smile.

Stan grinned. "Sorry about

that," he said. "I always test my spooks at this time of night. I suppose you saw my bat?"

Ricky and Zedex nodded. Stan sighed and then grinned.

"I'm afraid I've had a little bit of trouble with that bat," he said. "Its direction-control isn't working too well. I'll have to check it."

"Probably a faulty magnetic-bearing sensor," said Zedex helpfully.

Stan scratched his chin and regarded Zedex thoughtfully.

"I'm pretty good at making robots," he said, "but you, Zedex, are the best robot I've ever seen."

He turned to Ricky. "Your uncle must be very clever, Ricky."

"He is," said Ricky proudly. "Zedex took some pictures of your bat last night and we found out it was a robot. Uncle Jack thought it might have been made by a nasty man

called Professor Felonius, but I'm glad he was wrong."

Stan gave a start.

"Felonius? I met him! He came to see me yesterday. Offered me some money for my robots."

"What did you say to him?" gasped Ricky.

"I told him I would never sell them. He got very angry and left."

Zedex flashed a picture of a surly-looking man on his face-screen. "This is Felonius," he said.

Stan nodded. "That's him. Nasty-looking customer."

Ricky frowned. "You had better be careful, Stan," he said. "Uncle Jack has tangled with him in the past. He is not a nice person."

"I can take care of myself," grinned Stan. "Now, would you like to have a quick look at the rest of my spooks?"

"Yes!" said Ricky delightedly.

The inside of the truck was like a workshop. At the far end was a table piled high with an assortment of half-finished robots. Ricky could see bats' wings, scaly claws, webbed feet and grinning skulls all lying together in a jumble.

Beside this was a bench laden with tools. The most amazing things, however, were

the finished robot-spooks which hung on rails down both sides of the truck.

Ghosts, bats, monsters and creepy-crawlies of all shapes, sizes and colours stared at Ricky and Zedex with unblinking glass eyes.

Ricky shook his head and whistled.

"Terrific, Stan! They all look so spooky!"

"You bet!" he chortled. "But you should see them in my Haunted House at the fair. They are twice as spooky there!"

"Uncle Jack would love to see these," said Ricky.

"Bring him round tomorrow morning," said Stan. "We can talk robots."

Zedex nodded seriously.

"It's a fascinating subject," he said. "My favourite, in fact."

Uncle Jack was relieved to see them.

"Thank goodness you're safe! Where have you been?" he cried.

Quickly Ricky explained about Stan and his spooks and the invitation to visit the workshop. He also told his uncle about Professor Felonius.

Uncle Jack frowned. "Stan seems to be a nice person," he said. "I hope Felonius doesn't do anything nasty. We must go and see Stan tomorrow. Perhaps I can give him some advice."

After breakfast next morning the three of them piled into Uncle Jack's little car and headed for the place where the trucks were parked. When they got there, however, Stan's HAUNTED HOUSE truck was nowhere to be seen.

"But he said he'd be here!" said Ricky.

"I'll go and ask someone about him," said Uncle Jack.

Ricky and Zedex stayed in the car as Uncle Jack talked to the owner of the funfair, Mrs Lee.

She was a tall, thin woman with a pleasant face and long dark hair.

"Don't know where Stan has gone," she said. "But he had better hurry back, because we're leaving here soon."

"When did he go?" asked Uncle Jack.

"Oh, it must have been early this morning, before it got

light," said Mrs Lee. "Nobody saw him, which is strange, because we have all been up since the crack of dawn."

Uncle Jack thanked her and went back to the car, frowning.

"It doesn't feel right," he said. "Why would Stan leave so early without telling anyone?"

He turned to Zedex.

"Is it possible for you to pick up any signals from Stan's robots, Zedex?"

Zedex touched some buttons on his console.

"I'll try, Professor Brown," he said.

Zedex's face-screen went blank and nothing happened for a few seconds. Then a road-map appeared on the screen with a faint point of light blinking on and off beside one of the roads.

"I've got a reading," said Zedex. "A lot of powerful batteries all in one place."

"That must be Stan's truck!" cried Ricky.

His uncle looked at the road-map and started the engine. "And I know where it is!" he exclaimed. "Let's go!"

Chapter Four

Uncle Jack's little car sped through the countryside.

"The signal is getting stronger," said Zedex. "We are almost at the place!"

They had turned on to a narrow country lane when Zedex suddenly said, "There!" and pointed to a large house standing behind a high stone wall.

Uncle Jack stopped the car opposite the wrought-iron gates and they looked up the driveway. Through the railings they could just see the back of Stan's truck parked at the side of the house.

There was a sign attached to one of the gateposts which said:

LEO'S MECHANICAL TOYS.
WORKSHOP:

SPARES & REPAIRS.

ENJOYMENT FOR
ALL AGES.

LEO IS FUN!

Uncle Jack sat back in his seat and sighed.

"It looks like we've come on a wild-goose chase," he said. "Stan is probably here to get some spare parts for his robots. We've been worried for nothing."

He started the engine again.

"Let's go back, Ricky. Mrs Lee told me where the funfair is going, so we'll visit Stan there this evening. OK?"

Ricky nodded. "I suppose so, Uncle Jack," he said.

His uncle put the car into gear and began to move off, but Ricky suddenly shouted,

"Wait!"

The car lurched to a halt.

"What is it, Ricky?" asked Uncle Jack.

Ricky pointed at the sign on the gatepost.

"LEO IS FUN," he breathed, wide-eyed. "It's an anagram, Uncle Jack! If you rearrange the letters, it spells FELONIUS!"

His uncle's eyes opened

wide in amazement.

"You're right, Ricky! Smart thinking! That's just typical of Felonius's sense of humour. This place could be his laboratory. He must have kidnapped Stan to find out about his robots."

"What can we do, Uncle Jack? Call the police?"

His uncle frowned.

"Not at the moment, Ricky," he said slowly. "After all, we could be wrong."

He thought for a moment, then said, "Look, both of you stay here. I will go up to the house and find out what is really happening. If it turns out that Stan has been kidnapped, then we can call the police."

He drove the little car off the road and parked it in a field behind a hedge.

"Won't be long," he said, and crossed the road towards the house.

Ricky watched his uncle's progress anxiously.

He and Zedex lost sight of him for a few seconds as he crept through the gate into the driveway, but then saw him again as he stole up to Stan's truck.

Then everything happened at once.

Professor Felonius and his two henchmen came running out of the house. The two men

grabbed Uncle Jack and bundled him into the back of the truck as Professor Felonius started the engine. Then they ran down the driveway, opened the gates and jumped into the cab of the truck as Professor Felonius drove it through.

The truck swung out into the lane and picked up speed.

It passed Ricky and Zedex in their hiding-place in a cloud of diesel fumes.

Ricky and Zedex leapt out of the car.

"Quick, Ricky," said Zedex urgently. "We must follow them. I have a plan!"

Ricky climbed aboard the little seat and Zedex shot straight up into the air. He clung on to Zedex for dear life as the robot flew at top speed in pursuit of the truck. The rushing wind threatened to pluck him from Zedex's back,

they were going so fast.
Luckily, the headlong dash
only lasted a few minutes.

Ricky felt Zedex's speed slowing and looked down.

They were right above the truck. It swayed and bumped as it roared along the narrow lane.

Zedex swooped lower and hovered inches above its roof.

He tapped a button on his computer-console and pointed a finger at the roof.

"Are you going to use your laser-beam, Zedex?" shouted Ricky.

Zedex nodded and an intense beam of light suddenly shot from his fingertip.

Twenty seconds later he had cut out a square section of the roof and Ricky peered inside.

Down below he saw the faces of Stan and Uncle Jack looking up anxiously.

"Be careful, Ricky!" cried Uncle Jack.

"I'm OK, Uncle Jack!" Ricky yelled. "Zedex says he has a plan to help you!"

Zedex looked into the opening too. "Give me the spooks' remote-control, please, Stan," he called.

Stan threw it up and Zedex caught it.

"Thank you. Now, both of you hold on to something solid. I'm going to try something."

Chapter Five

Zedex hovered steadily over the truck, keeping pace with it, and touched some buttons on the remote-control device.

A few seconds later, two of Stan's spooks rose out of the hole in the roof and hovered beside them.

"What are you going to do, Zedex?" Ricky shouted above the roar of the truck's engine. He eyed the ghosts curiously.

"Get Felonius to stop the truck, I hope!" Zedex shouted back, moving the little joystick which stuck up from the middle of the remote-control.

The two ghosts whirled round, their white sheets flapping, and swooped towards the front of the truck.

Professor Felonius and his two henchmen started in surprise as the spooks suddenly appeared in front of them and draped themselves over the windscreen.

"What's going on?" shrieked Felonius. "I can't see a thing!"

In a panic, he stamped on the brake. The truck skidded wildly over the grass verge into a field and screeched to a halt.

Zedex landed near the truck and Ricky dismounted.

The robot then used the remote-control again and the rest of Stan's spooks came flying out of the hole in the roof, just as Felonius and his two cronies clambered out of the cab. Professor Felonius saw the remote-control in Zedex's hand and scowled.

"So it was you!" he snarled and lunged forward. "Give that to me!"

Zedex coolly twiddled the joystick, however, and

suddenly Felonius and his henchmen were surrounded by flapping ghosts, fluttering bats, dancing skeletons and leaping ghouls.

Felonius tripped over three little green monsters who were jumping around his feet and fell flat on the ground.

His two cronies staggered about with their hands flailing, trying to knock down the spooks which flapped in their faces.

"Quickly, Ricky!" hissed Zedex urgently. "Get the truck keys and release Stan and your uncle!"

Ricky dashed off.

Zedex saw that Felonius was getting to his feet and put part two of his plan into action.

He moved the joystick once more and suddenly the spooks stopped whirling around the two men and flew off along the road. Professor Felonius howled with rage.

"Bring those robots back!" he roared. Turning to his cronies, he shouted, "Ned! Get after them! Don't let them out of your sight! Bill. . . !" he spun round and pointed at Zedex. "Get that remote-control!"

Before Bill could rush forward, Zedex held up the remote-control in his left hand and blasted it with a laser-beam from his right.

Bill stopped short and gawped at the smoking, melted plastic.

"You've broken it!" he gasped. He turned to his boss, mouth hanging open. "He's broken it, Professor!"

Felonius's eyes narrowed in anger, but before he could say anything there was a scuffling noise behind him and he and Bill suddenly found themselves covered by a huge net.

Ricky had managed to free Uncle Jack and Stan and they had crept up on Felonius and Bill unawares.

They now ran round the

fuming and struggling pair, tangling them up hopelessly in the net and finally tying the loose ends into a tight knot.

Felonius and Bill struggled and cursed, but were completely trapped.

Uncle Jack laughed and shook his head.

"Oh dear! When will you ever learn, Professor Felonius? Crime doesn't pay!" He laughed again.

Meanwhile, Stan had fetched his spare remote-control and recalled his spooks.

"That was clever, destroying the remote-control, Zedex," said Ricky admiringly. "But how did you know that Stan had a spare?"

"I noticed it when we visited

his truck last night," smiled Zedex.

"You are pretty smart, you know," said Ricky with a laugh.

"He certainly is!" beamed Uncle Jack, clapping Zedex on the shoulder.

Stan added his praises. So much so, in fact, that the robot's face-screen became pink with embarrassment again.

Stan thanked Ricky too, and when he had made sure that all of his spooks were safely stowed away, he turned to Uncle Jack.

"I've got a lot to learn from you about robots, Jack," he said. "We must have a chin-wag some time."

Ricky's uncle smiled. "We certainly must, Stan," he said. "It is not only Zedex's favourite subject. It is mine too!"

Before they left, Uncle Jack went over to Professor Felonius and Bill, who now sat glumly but quietly at the edge of the field, completely swathed in the tight net.

"Your chum will be back soon, Professor," he smiled. "He'll set you free. All I can

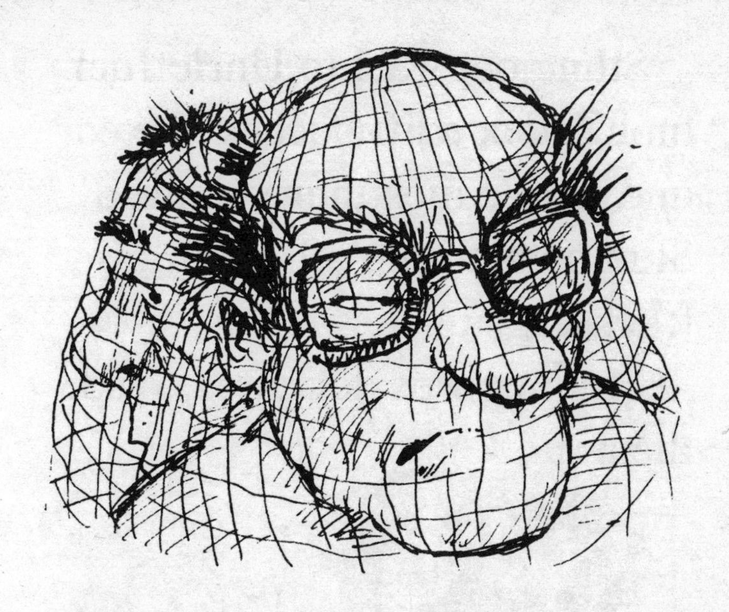

say is, let's hope we don't meet again."

Felonius glared after him angrily as he walked away and muttered under his breath, "You can hope all you like, Professor Brown . . . but we will most certainly meet again. Oh yes!"

Stan gave Ricky, Uncle Jack and Zedex a lift back to the car and Uncle Jack then followed Stan back to the other funfair trucks.

Mrs Lee was delighted to see them.

"It wouldn't have been much of a funfair without your spooks, Stan," she said when she heard the whole story. "We'll make sure that you get proper protection from now on."

She thanked Ricky, Uncle Jack and Zedex for their help and Stan gave them free passes to the funfair for a whole year before waving goodbye.

Soon after they got back to Uncle Jack's house, Ricky's mum and dad arrived to take him home.

"Did you have a nice time,

Ricky?" asked his mum.

"Terrific!" said Ricky.

"Well, the quiet life in the country certainly seems to agree with you!" said his dad.

There was a slight pause as Ricky, Uncle Jack and Zedex looked at one another, then all three burst into gales of laughter.